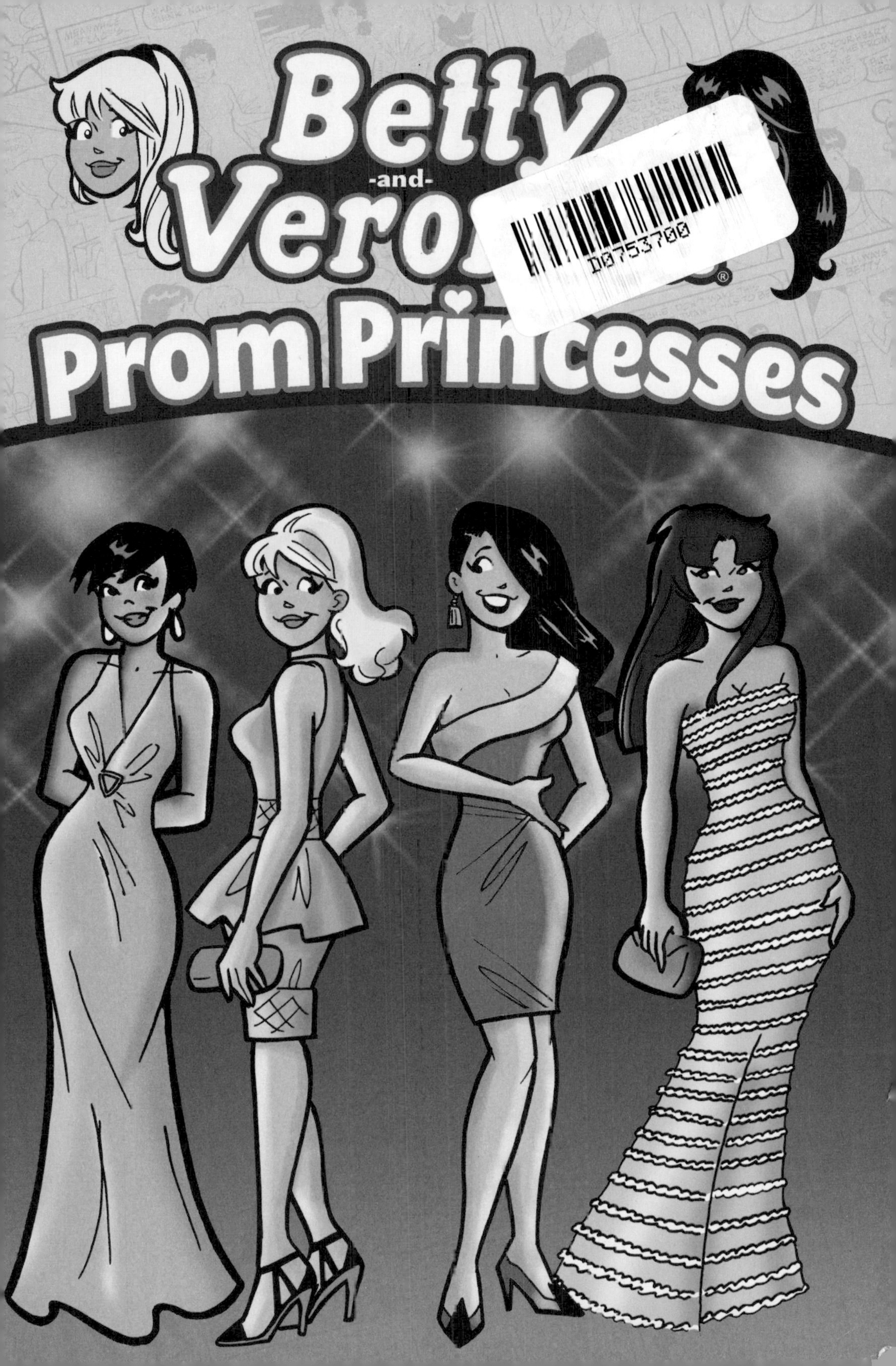
Betty
-and-
Vero
Prom Princesses

Betty -and- Veronica® Prom Princesses

Archie & Friends All-Stars Vol. 19,
BETTY & VERONICA: PROM PRINCESSES
Published by Archie Comic Publications, Inc.
325 Fayette Avenue, Mamaroneck, New York 10543-2318.

 Printed in U.S.A.
FIRST PRINTING.

ISBN: 978-1-936975-30-3

Publisher / Co-CEO: Jon Goldwater
Co-CEO: Nancy Silberkleit
President: Mike Pellerito
Co-President / Editor-In-Chief: Victor Gorelick
Senior Vice President – Sales & Business Development: Jim Sokolowski
Senior Vice-President – Publishing & Operations: Harold Buchholz
Executive Director of Editorial: Paul Kaminski
Project Coordinator & Book Design: Joe Morciglio
Production Manager: Stephen Oswald
Production: Jon Gray, Tito Peña
Proofreader / Editorial Assistant: Jamie Lee Rotante

Betty -and- Veronica®

Prom Princesses

STORIES BY:

DAN PARENT

BARBARA SLATE

ARTWORK BY:

DAN PARENT

JEFF SHULTZ

STAN GOLDBERG

BOB SMITH

RICH KOSLOWSKI

JIM AMASH

JON D'AGOSTINO

JACK MORELLI

TERESA DAVIDSON

BARRY GROSSMAN

DIGIKORE STUDIOS

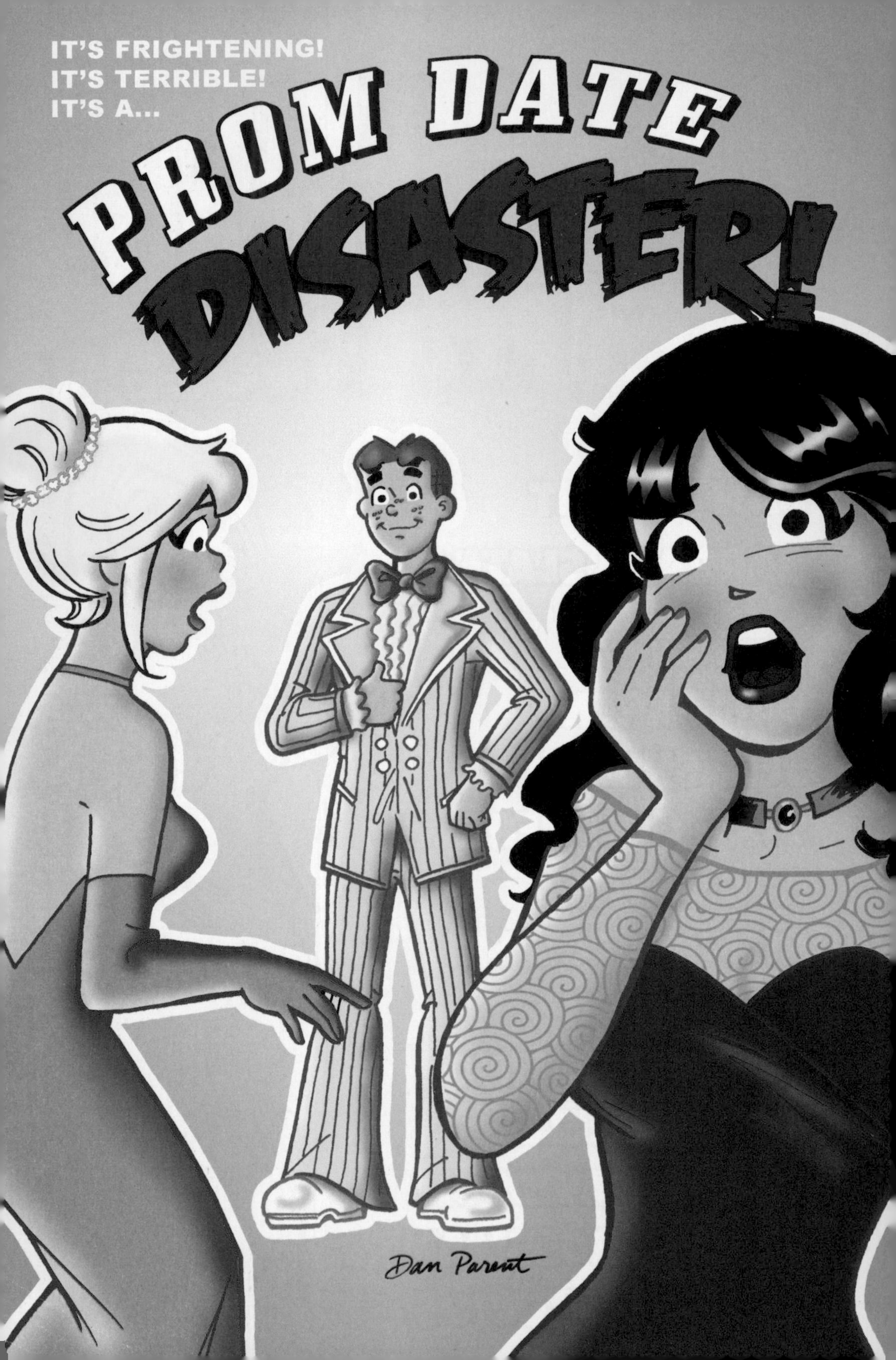
IT'S FRIGHTENING!
IT'S TERRIBLE!
IT'S A...
PROM DATE
DISASTER!
Dan Parent

Betty and Veronica in PROM DATE DISASTERS
BETTY, DO YOU REMEMBER SOME OF THE PROM DATE DISASTERS WE'VE HAD?!
I WAS JUST THINKING ABOUT ONE, VERONICA! REMEMBER THE LIMOUSINE FIASCO FROM LAST YEAR?
RIGHT! THAT WAS WHEN OUR LIMO BROKE DOWN!
AND WE HAD TO RIDE IN THE BACK OF MOOSE'S PICK-UP TRUCK!
1

WHICH WOULDN'T HAVE BEEN SO BAD IF WE HADN'T HIT THAT POTHOLE!
THUD
AND THAT MUD PUDDLE!
REMEMBER THE YEAR OF "THE GLADIOLA"?
HOW COULD I FORGET? THERE WAS A BEE IN THAT GLADIOLA CORSAGE MOOSE GAVE MIDGE!
IT STUNG HER RIGHT ON THE NOSE!
YEOW!
IT PROBABLY WOULD NEVER HAVE HAPPENED IF CHEAPO MOOSE HADN'T PICKED THE GLADIOLA FROM MIDGE'S GARDEN!

YOU WEREN'T ANYWHERE NEAR THE MESS JUGHEAD MADE OF ETHEL ONE YEAR!
OH, I FORGOT ABOUT THAT ONE!
JUGHEAD POLISHED OFF A WHOLE BUFFET TABLE!
AND ETHEL FORCED HIM TO SWING DANCE!
THAT WAS TOO MUCH! EVEN FOR HIS STOMACH!
YUCK! HE GOT SICK!
AND ALL OVER HER DRESS!
LET'S CHANGE THE SUBJECT!!
REMEMBER THE BIG HAIR FIASCO?!
OH, DEAR! THAT WAS EMBARRASSING!
WHY MARIA PERMED HER HAIR LIKE THAT I'LL NEVER KNOW!

BUT THAT BIG DO GOT CAUGHT ON THE BUTTON OF FRANKIE'S SLEEVE!
AND WHEN HE FLUNG HIS ARM AROUND...
SHE SLAMMED INTO MR. WEATHERBEE AND MS. GRUNDY SHARING A DANCE!
NOT TO MENTION SHE TORE THE DRESS, TOO!
AND SHE WAS NOT AWARE OF IT UNTIL REGGIE POINTED IT OUT!
IN HIS OWN SPECIAL STYLE!
THIS YEAR EVERYTHING WILL GO GREAT!
IT HAS TO! WE'VE PAID OUR DUES IN THE PAST!
WE'RE DUE TO HAVE A SMOOTH EVENING THIS YEAR!!

WE CAN'T GO WRONG WITH THESE GOWNS!
WE DO LOOK GREAT IF I DO SAY SO MYSELF!
AND WE'RE SMART TO BOTH AGREE TO GO WITH ARCHIE TONIGHT!
Oh, HE'S HERE!!
DING DONG
HI, GIRLS! READY TO GO?!
GAK!!
THANKS TO HIS TUX, WE'VE GOT YET ANOTHER PROM DISASTER TO TALK ABOUT!
THERE'S ALWAYS NEXT YEAR!
the END

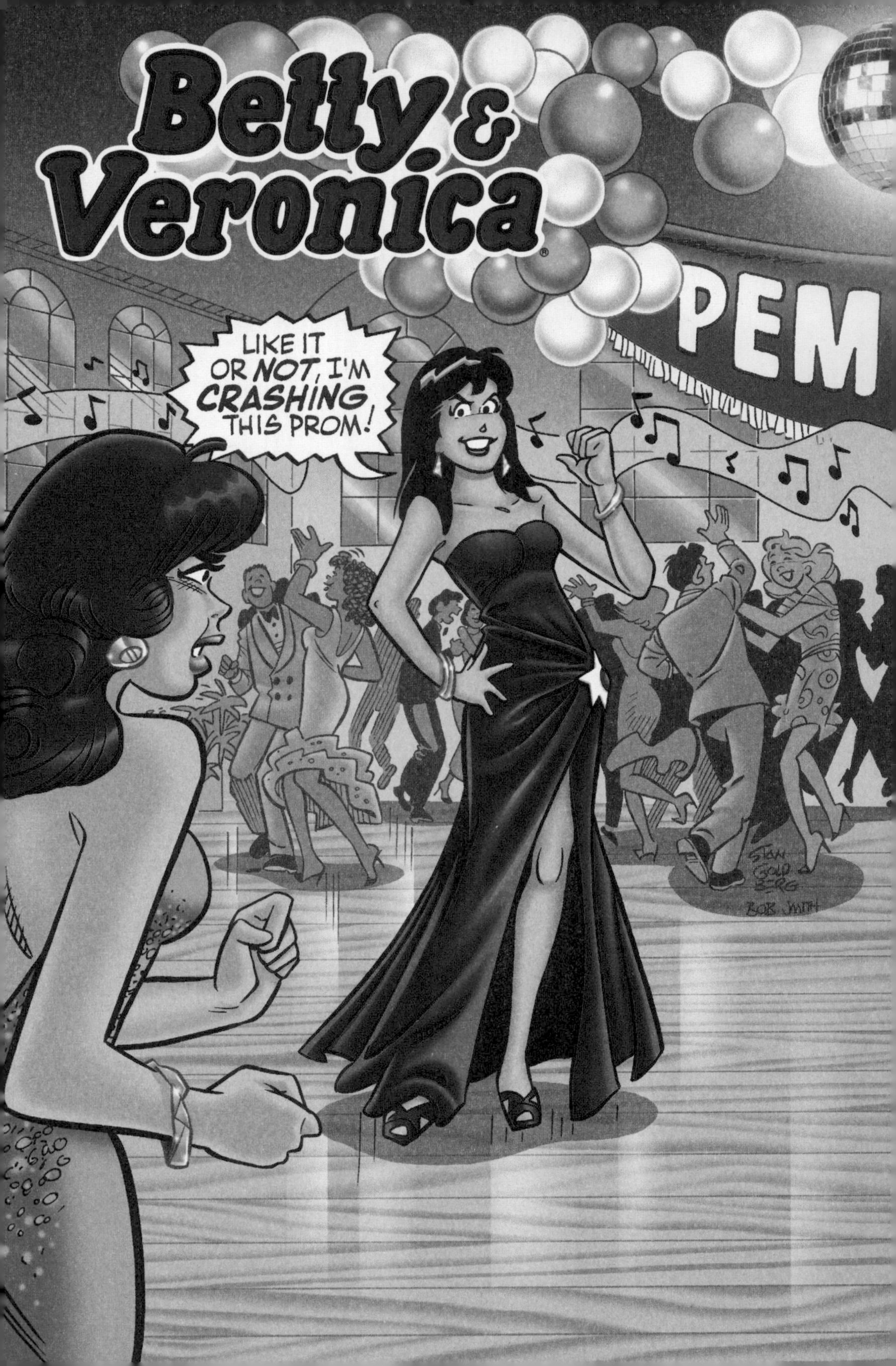
Betty & Veronica®
LIKE IT OR NOT, I'M CRASHING THIS PROM!
PEM
STAN GOLDBERG
BOB SMITH

The PROM-CRASHERS!
BRO
I'M CRASHING THIS PROM!
STAN GOLDBERG
BOB SMITH

Veronica IN THE PROM CRASHERS
THAT DRESS LOOKS JUST GORGEOUS ON YOU, VERONICA!
WELL, IT'S ALL BECAUSE OF YOU, GINGER!
PIZZA
GLITZ MAGAZINE
1
SCRIPT: DAN PARENT
PENCILS: STAN GOLDBERG
INKING: RICH KOSLOWSKI
LETTERING: JACK MORELLI
COLORING: BARRY GROSSMAN
MANAGING EDITOR: MIKE PELLERITO
EDITOR/EDITOR-IN-CHIEF: VICTOR GORELICK

AFTER ALL, YOU DESIGNED IT!
WELL, I NEED SOME GREAT PROM FASHIONS FOR "GLITZ" MAGAZINE!
AFTER ALL, WE'RE PUTTING OUT OUR HUGE PROM ISSUE!*
GLITZ
*GINGER LOPEZ IS A TEEN EDITOR AND FASHION DESIGNER FOR "GLITZ".
THANKS FOR LETTING US MODEL YOUR FASHION DESIGNS!
WE WANT REAL GIRLS IN OUR MAGA-ZINE!
GLITZ
AND YOU'RE THE "REALEST" GIRLS I KNOW!
BUT REMEMBER-- I WANT YOUR GREATEST PROM STORIES, TOO!

NO PROBLEM THERE!
WE'VE GOT PLENTY OF THEM!
LATER...
LET ME SEE... WHAT SORT OF PROM MEMORIES CAN I SHARE?
I REMEMBER OUR FIRST JUNIOR PROM...
RIVERDALE JUNIOR HIGH PROM
"NEITHER BETTY NOR I WAS ALLOWED TO GO ON A REAL DATE YET...
"SO WE BOTH WENT AFTER ARCHIE AT THAT PROM...
"WE ALMOST SPLIT THE POOR GUY IN TWO!"

"AND THIS WENT ON FOR THE NEXT PROM...
"AND THE NEXT..."
THEN, ONCE WE WERE ALLOWED TO DATE, THE WHOLE DYNAMIC CHANGED!
"WILL HE ASK ME, OR WILL HE ASK BETTY?
?
"EITHER WAY, ONE OF US ENDS UP BROKEN-HEARTED!"
ARCHIE
R
NOW THAT I THINK ABOUT IT, THE PROM IS ALWAYS STRESSFUL!

WE WENT AROUND ON PINS AND NEEDLES HOPING TO GET ASKED OUT... WITH SOMEONE ALWAYS LEFT OUT IN THE COLD!
LATER...
SO, GIRLS... DO YOU HAVE ANY THOUGHTS ON THE PROM?
YES! I'VE COME TO THE CONCLUSION WE HAVE BECOME WAY TOO STRESSED ABOUT THIS!
I AGREE!
ME TOO!
WOW! I CAME TO THE SAME CONCLUSION!
I'M TIRED OF SITTING AROUND AND WAITING TO BE ASKED OUT!
I'M HAVING NONE OF THAT!!

THAT'S WHY I WENT AHEAD AND ASKED DILTON MYSELF! WHY DO WE HAVE TO WAIT FOR A BOY TO ASK US?
RIVERD
HIGH SCHO
WELL, WE'VE BOTH ASKED ARCHIE BEFORE...
BUT ONCE AGAIN, ONE OF US IS ALWAYS LEFT OUT AND DE-JECTED!
LET'S MAKE A PACT! NEITHER OF US WILL GO WITH ARCHIE THIS YEAR!
WELL, uh... OKAY! LET'S DO IT!!
SEE? NOW THERE'S NO STRESS! AT LEAST WHERE ARCHIE IS CONCERNED!
6

NOW WE'LL HAVE TO FIGURE OUT WHO WE'RE GOING TO ASK!
WELL, I'LL OBVIOUSLY BE GOING WITH MY MOOSE!
AND CHUCK FOR ME, OF COURSE!
MIDGE
I DON'T KNOW WHO I'M GOING WITH YET!
THAT MAKES THREE OF US, ETHEL!
ALL RIGHT, GIRLS! LET'S TAKE SOME NOTES ON PROM LIFE! THIS IS GOING TO BE A GREAT ISSUE!
LATER...
VERONIKINS! GUESS WHAT? I'VE MADE MY DECISION!
I'D LIKE YOU TO BE MY DATE FOR THE PROM THIS YEAR!

NO.
EXCUSE ME?
I SAID "NO."
B-BUT WHY?
BETTY AND I ARE TAKING A BREAK FROM THE STRESS THIS YEAR!
WE'RE KEEPING OUR OPTIONS OPEN!
HMPH!! WE'LL JUST SEE ABOUT THAT!
SOON...
WHAT?! YOU'RE TURNING ME DOWN?!
ARCHIE, YOU KNOW I'D LOVE TO GO WITH YOU...
BUT I CAN'T!
WE'RE TAKING A BREAK THIS YEAR!

AWWW, C'MON... YOU CAN CHANGE YOUR MIND FOR LI'L OL' ARCHIEKINS... CAN'T YOU?
WELL-L-L...
BETTY! SNAP OUT OF IT!!
SORRY, ARCHIE!
DRATS!
AT VERONICA'S...
TIME TO LOOK THROUGH THESE PHOTOS FROM OUR LAST FEW PROMS!
ALBUM
HERE'S A GREAT PHOTO OF ARCHIE AND I--
THEN THAT SHE-DEVIL CHERYL BLOSSOM REARS HER UGLY HEAD!

THEN SHE HORNED IN ON BETTY THAT ONE TIME!
THEN THERE WAS LAST YEAR WHEN I FLEW TO PARIS TO GET A DESIGNER GOWN!
"AND CHERYL WENT OUT OF HER WAY TO DUPLICATE MY DESIGN AND UPSTAGE ME!"
"AND SHE WENT TO THE PROM WITH REGGIE, WHO SHE HAD HER CLAWS IN AT THE TIME!
"ONLY TO PIT ARCHIE AND REGGIE AGAINST EACH OTHER, CAUSING TROUBLE AGAIN!"
HEY! I'M NOTICING A TREND HERE!

CHERYL BLOSSOM HAS RUINED, OR TRIED TO RUIN, EVERY PROM SINCE HIGH SCHOOL BEGAN!
AND EVEN THOUGH SHE LIVES IN PEMBROOKE, SHE ALWAYS CRASHES OUR PROMS!
THAT GIRL IS A PROM CRASHER!
?
THE NEXT DAY...
GIRLS! I DECIDED TO TAKE MY FATE INTO MY OWN HANDS!
I GOT MYSELF A PROM DATE!
GREAT!
WHO DID YOU ASK?
ARCHIE!

WHAT?!
WELL, SINCE YOU TWO ARE TAKING A BREAK FROM HIM... I FIGURED, WHY NOT?
YOU'RE NOT MAD, ARE YOU?
OF COURSE NOT! WE WANT YOU BOTH TO HAVE A GREAT TIME!
THANKS, GIRLS!
SO... DID YOU GIRLS HEAR ABOUT ETHEL AND ME?
YES! WE HOPE YOU HAVE A GOOD TIME!
IT'LL WORK OUT FOR THE BEST!
I'LL GO WITH ETHEL, BUT I'LL JUST DANCE THE NIGHT AWAY WITH EACH OF YOU!
EVERY-BODY WINS!
YEAH, EVERYBODY...
EXCEPT ETHEL!
12

THERE'S ONLY ONE THING WE CAN DO...
NOT ATTEND THE PROM!
WHAT ?!!
WITH US THERE, ARCHIE WILL IGNORE ETHEL!
AND JUST BEING THERE WITH ARCHIE WILL BE STRESSFUL, ANYWAY!
THE BEST BET IS TO JUST STAY AWAY FROM THE PROM!
BUT I DON'T WANT TO MISS THE PROM!
WELL, WE'LL MISS THIS PROM... BUT WE'LL STILL GO TO A PROM!
?!
13

WHAT ARE YOU TALKING ABOUT?
WE'RE GOING TO THE PEMBROOKE PROM!
WHY WOULD WE DO THAT?!
IT'LL BE A GREAT ANGLE FOR THE PROM STORY FOR "GLITZ" MAGAZINE!
SORT OF LIKE AN INVESTIGATIVE STORY ON PROMS!
Hmmm... INTERESTING!
MATH TEST SCORES
PLUS, CHERYL HAS CRASHED EVERY PROM WE'VE HAD!
I THINK IT'S TIME THE SHOE WAS ON THE OTHER FOOT!
MOOSE
R

THIS COULD BE FUN!
PLUS, WITH A NEW CROWD OF PEOPLE, WE WON'T HAVE THOSE SAME PRESSURES WE USUALLY HAVE!
NAMELY, ARCHIE!
YOU GOT IT!!
SO...
YOU GIRLS ARE GOING TO CRASH THE PEMBROOKE PROM?!
COOL!
MAKE SURE YOU TAKE NOTES AND BRING YOUR CAMERA!
I'LL BE TAKING VIDEO ON THIS STORY!
I CAN'T WAIT TO SEE THE LOOK ON CHERYL'S FACE!
WAIT! ARE YOU SURE SHE'LL BE THERE?

YES! I TALKED TO HER BROTHER JASON!
SHE'S ATTENDING THE PROM WITH HER NEW BOYFRIEND, GEORGE!*
*READ ABOUT GEORGE IN B&V DOUBLE DIGEST #165!
LET'S GO!
I HAVE A LOT OF PREPARING TO DO!
YOU LOOK SENSATIONAL, BETTY!!
AS DO YOU, MY FELLOW PROM-CRASHER!
16

YOU GIRLS LOOK GREAT!!
WHO ARE YOUR DATES TONIGHT?
NOBODY!!
AREN'T YOU GOING TO THE RIVERDALE HIGH PROM?
NOPE!
Huh?!
IT'S NOT WORTH TRYING TO FIGURE THEM OUT, HIRAM... YOU SHOULD KNOW THAT BY NOW!
AT THE RIVER-DALE PROM...
ARCHIE, AREN'T YOU HAVING FUN?
OF COURSE, ETHEL...

YOU KEEP LOOKING OVER YOUR SHOULDER!
YOU'RE LOOKING FOR BETTY AND VERONICA, AREN'T YOU?
WELLLL...
I UNDERSTAND... BUT THEY'RE NOT GOING TO BE HERE TONIGHT!
WHY NOT?!
BECAUSE THEY'RE GOING TO THE PEMBROOKE PROM!
WHAT?! WHO ASKED THEM?!
NOBODY!
THEY'RE CRASHING THE PROM!
COOL, HUH?
THAT PEMBROOKE CROWD IS BRUTAL! THEY DON'T KNOW WHAT THEY'RE IN FOR!!
18

THOSE GIRLS ARE TOUGH! THEY CAN HANDLE THEM-SELVES!
I'VE GOT TO GO AFTER THEM!
ME AND MY BIG MOUTH!
NOW I'M DATELESS AGAIN!
SO...
HERE WE ARE, BETTY!
PEMBROOKE HIGH
PROM TONITE
ARE WE READY TO GO?
I'M KIND OF NERVOUS!
BUT READY!
HELLO THERE!
I.D.'S PLEASE!
TICKETS
THESE ARE RIVERDALE HIGH I.D.'S!
THESE WON'T WORK HERE!

WHAT?!
IF YOU DON'T HAVE A PEMBROOKE I.D., THE ONLY WAY YOU CAN GET IN IS AS A GUEST!
WHAT NOW?
I HAVE THE SOLUTION! I'LL CALL JASON BLOSSOM!
HELLO, JASON?
COULD YOU MEET US OUT FRONT!?
BETTY! VERONICA! WHAT ARE YOU DOING HERE?
PEMB
HIGH
WE NEED TO GET IN! BUT WE NEED AN INVITE FROM YOU!
AND WHAT'S IN IT FOR ME?
WELL... HOW ABOUT A COUPLE OF SLOW DANCES?
WELL... THAT'S A START!

THEN THERE'S THE LOOK OF SHOCK AND DISGUST ON YOUR SISTER'S FACE WHEN SHE SEES US!
TWO GUEST TICKETS PLEASE!
THANKS, JASON!
MAKE IT WORTH MY WHILE! SHAKE MY SISTER UP GOOD!
THERE SHE IS!
DJ KING
SHOULD WE SAY HELLO?
NO... LET'S KEEP A LOW PROFILE AT FIRST!
LET'S MINGLE A BIT!
ATTENTION, EVERYONE!!
ESPECIALLY MY SISTER CHERYL!
I'D LIKE TO WELCOME MY TWO SPECIAL RIVERDALE GUESTS...
!
!
21

VERONICA LODGE AND BETTY COOPER!
WHAT?! HOW DARE YOU CRASH A PEMBROOKE PROM?!
I'M SCARED!
PUFF! PUFF! DON'T WORRY, GIRLS! I'M COMING! ARCHIE TO THE RESCUE!!
PEMBROOKE HIGH
PROM TONITE
PROM TONITE

HOW DARE YOU CRASH A PEMBROOKE PROM! YOU'VE GOT A LOT OF NERVE!
WHAT ARE YOU TALKING ABOUT? YOU'VE CRASHED OUR PROMS FOR YEARS!
THAT WAS BECAUSE OF ARCHIE!
HE USUALLY INVITED ME!
WELL... YOUR BROTHER JASON INVITED US!
GRRR! THAT FIGURES!!

YOU'RE JUST DOING THAT TO TICK ME OFF!
WORKS FOR ME!
WHATEVER! JUST STAY OUT OF MY WAY!!
WITH PLEASURE!
BETTY! VERONICA!! I'M HERE!!
Wha? WHO?
PEMBROOKE
Oh, BROTHER!!
IT'S OUR KNIGHT IN SHINING ARMOR!
HEY! GET BACK HERE!!
YOU CAN'T COME IN HERE UNLESS YOU'RE INVITED!
IT'S OKAY!
4

HE'S INVITED!
hmph!
THANKS!
ARCHIE! WHAT ARE YOU DOING HERE? YOU'RE SUPPOSED TO BE WITH ETHEL!
WHEN I HEARD ABOUT YOU TWO BEING HERE IN PEMBROOKE, I GOT WORRIED!
WHY? DON'T YOU THINK WE CAN HANDLE THESE PEMBROOKE SNOBS?!
AND WE DON'T NEED YOU TO WATCH OVER US!
SO FEEL FREE TO LEAVE!
THAT'S OKAY! YOU'RE HERE, ARCHIE... YOU MIGHT AS WELL STAY!
I'LL EVEN HAVE A DANCE WITH YOU!
Hmph!
5

Oh, GEORGE! IT'S JUST A DANCE! YOU KNOW I ONLY HAVE EYES FOR YOU!
WELLL... OKAY!
DJ KING
OKAY, BETTY! WHERE'S THAT DANCE YOU PROMISED ME?
LET'S GO!
WELL, THAT LEAVES US, GEORGE!
WANNA DANCE?
SURE!
I WANT TO TALK TO YOU, ANYWAY!
I HAVE TO KNOW! DOES CHERYL STILL HAVE A THING FOR ARCHIE?
I JUST WANT TO KNOW WHERE I STAND!
YOU'LL HAVE TO ASK HER! BUT I CAN TELL YOU ONE THING...
BROOK

WHENEVER WE COUNT HER OUT...
SHE ALWAYS FINDS A WAY BACK IN!
GOOD LUCK WITH HER!
YOU'RE GOING TO NEED IT!
?
WELL, GIRLS, SINCE WE'RE ALL HERE NOW...
WHO WANTS THE FIRST DANCE?
NEITHER! WE TOLD YOU, WE'RE HAVING AN ARCHIE-FREE PROM!!
BUT... BUT...
HI, RED!
Oh, HI, BECKY!
*BECKY'S ONE OF CHERYL'S FRIENDS WHO LIKES ARCHIE!

WILL YOU HAVE THIS DANCE WITH ME?
SURE!
LOOKS LIKE BECKY'S GOT HER CLAWS IN HIM!
GOOD! ARCHIE ISN'T OUR PROBLEM TONIGHT!
HI, GIRLS!
WAIT! I KNOW YOU GUYS FROM SOMEWHERE...
I GOT IT!!
YOU WERE BOTH IN THE RUNNING IN THE CONTEST TO BE CHERYL'S BOYFRIEND!*
*SEE B&V DOUBLE DIGESTS #161 -165!
YEAH, I'M BRANDON!
I'M AUSTIN!
PEMBRO
YOU CAN CALL US CHERYL'S REJECTS!
YOU'RE THE BEST-LOOKING REJECTS I'VE EVER SEEN!
8

MAY WE HAVE A DANCE?
SURE!
PEM
SOON...
THINGS SEEM TO BE GOING NICELY...
THIS MAY TURN OUT TO BE A NICE EVENING AFTER ALL!
LET ME IN!
WHO'S THAT?
IT SOUNDS LIKE--
ETHEL!
WHERE IS HE? WHERE'S ARCHIE?!
YOU'RE NOT INVITED!
BACK OFF, SISTER!!

ARCHIE ANDREWS! HOW DARE YOU DESERT ME! I'M TIRED OF ALWAYS BEING LEFT OUT IN THE COLD!
AND I'M NOT GOING TO STAND FOR IT ANYMORE!
HE'S MINE, GIRLIE! AT LEAST FOR TONIGHT!
START DANCING!
YES, MA'AM!
WOW! LOOK AT ETHEL STICKING UP FOR HERSELF!
GOOD FOR HER!
MAY I COME IN?
WHY NOT?! THE REST OF RIVER-DALE IS HERE!
GINGER! WHAT'S UP?
I WANT TO CATCH ALL OF THIS ON TAPE!
PEMBR

PEMBROOKE
THIS WILL BE GREAT FOR MY ARTICLE IN "GLITZ"!
THIS IS RIDICULOUS!! YOU TOWNIES ARE BRINGING DOWN THIS WHOLE PROM!!
WHAT'S THAT?!
YOU'RE ON THE RECORD FOR "GLITZ" MAGAZINE!
Oh... uh... WELL... HELLO! MY, AREN'T YOU LOOKING LOVELY TODAY, GINGER!
OMIGOSH! LOOK!! THE REST OF THE GANG IS TRICKLING IN!!

WE WERE GETTING LONELY AT OUR PROM!
IT'S NOT THE SAME WITHOUT YOU GUYS!
PEMBROO
WE THOUGHT, IF YOU CAN CRASH PEMBROOKE'S PROM-- WE CAN, TOO!!
PEMBROOKE HIGH
PROM
PROM
SICKENING! SIMPLY SICKENING!!
HELLO, CHERYL!
HELLO, REGGIE.
ANOTHER ONE OF YOUR EX-BOYFRIENDS ??!
THEY'RE JUST CRAWLING OUT OF THE WOODWORK, AREN'T THEY?
WELL!
DON'T WORRY! I'VE MOVED ON!
GOOD LUCK, GEORGE! YOU'LL NEED IT!!
PEMBROOKE

SO, GIRLS! HOW'S THE NIGHT GOING?
WHAT'S THE REACTION BEEN?
WELL, WE HAD A LITTLE TROUBLE GETTING IN...
BUT THANKS TO JASON, WE GOT IN!
AND SO FAR, SO GOOD!
CHERYL HAS GEORGE NOW, SO THERE'S BEEN NO ARCHIE CONFLICT!
IN FACT, VERONICA AND I ARE HAVING FUN MEETING NEW PEOPLE AND DANCING THE NIGHT AWAY!
AND JASON, WHAT DO YOU THINK OF US "TOWNIES" INVADING YOUR PROM?
I'M VERY OPEN-MINDED!
ESPECIALLY WHEN IT COMES TO GORGEOUS TOWNIES LIKE YOU!

TELL ME ABOUT THIS FINE SCHOOL!
WE'RE ONE OF THE OLDEST, MOST PROMINENT SCHOOLS IN THE STATE!
WE'RE ONE OF THE FEW OLD SCHOOLS WITH AN OLYMPIC STYLE SWIMMING POOL... UNDER THE GYM FLOOR!
I'VE SEEN THOSE IN OLD MOVIES!
THAT'S RIGHT! I BELIEVE THIS LEVER OPENS THE FLOOR!
POOL
FLONK
OOPS!
POOL
OMIGOSH!!
THE FLOOR'S OPENING!!
I--I CAN'T MOVE THE LEVER BACK!
UH-OH!
14

I THINK I NEED TO SIT DOWN!
IT FEELS LIKE THE ROOM'S SPINNING!
LOOK OUT!
WH-WHAT'S GOING ON?!
THE FLOOR'S OPENING UP!!
WOO!
EEEEEE
BETTY!! HELP!
I'VE GOT YOU, RON!

BUT WHO'S GOT ME?!
ARCHIE TO THE RESCUE!
SEE?
I TOLD YOU I'D RESCUE YOU TONIGHT!
IT LOOKS LIKE THAT'S TRUE!
OH, ARCHIE--
--THINK FAST!!
PUSH
YIIII!
16

SPLOOSH
THAT'S JUST GREAT!
MY $2000 DRESS... RUINED!!
:sigh: SO IS MY $30 ONE.
HA! HA!!
I'M GLAD YOU GUYS CRASHED THIS PROM AFTER ALL!
I ALWAYS SAID YOU GIRLS WERE ALL WET!
17

HOW RIGHT I WAS!
oh, CHERYL?
YES, NUMBSKULL?
SHOVE
EEEEEE
SPLISH
GREAT! NOW WHAT?!
WELL... SHE IS MY DATE...
I MAY AS WELL JOIN HER!

SPLOOSH
I COULD USE A LITTLE COOLING OFF!
ME TOO!
SPLASH
IF YOU CAN'T BEAT 'EM, JOIN 'EM!
SPLOOSH
WE'RE THE *CHAPERONES*... AWWW... BUT WHAT THE HECK!

WHEE! THIS IS FUN!!
I-- I FORGOT! I CAN'T SWIM!!
PEMBROOKE
GINGER! THIS'LL GIVE YOU QUITE A STORY!
TO SAY THE LEAST!
WHO'S MISSING?
ME!
I HAVE TO WATCH THE FOOD!
IT MIGHT GET WET!
PEMBROOKE

ALL RIGHT, WE'VE HAD OUR FUN!
BUT WE HAVE TO CALL IT A NIGHT!
YOU KIDS BETTER GET HOME AND GET DRIED OFF!
AWWW! IT'S TOO EARLY!
I'M HUNGRY! IS THERE ANY PLACE OPEN FOR A BITE?
NO! PEMBROOKE SHUTS DOWN AROUND 8:00 P.M..!
WHAT A BORING TOWN YOU LIVE IN!!
I KNOW SOME-ONE WHO STAYS OPEN LATE!
OF COURSE!
FOLLOW US!
PEMBRO

I HATE PROM NIGHT! IT'S ALWAYS DEAD IN HERE!
HEY, POP!!
I SPOKE TOO SOON! WHAT HAPPENED TO ALL OF YOU?
POP'S
TODAY'S SPECIAL
IT'S A LONG STORY!
TELL ME LATER! I'LL FIRE UP THE GRILL!
POP'S
ALL IN ALL, IT WAS A FUN EVENING!
POP'S
IT'S TOO BAD ETHEL'S DATE WITH ARCHIE WAS DIS-RUPTED!
I DON'T THINK WE HAVE TO WORRY!
SHE'S WORKING THROUGH HER PAIN QUITE WELL!
END

PROM HERE TO Eternity!
Dan Parent

Betty and Veronica®
in
PROM HERE TO Eternity!
WHAT ARE YOU LOOKING AT, RON?
I'M JUST TRYING TO GET SOME IDEAS FOR A PROM DRESS!
Style through the DECADES
WELL, I CAN'T AFFORD TO BUY ONE! I'M MAKING MINE!
WOULDN'T IT BE NICE IF YOU COULD BE MORE LIKE BETTY!
MAKE MY OWN DRESS! THAT'S FUNNY!
SORRY! I THOUGHT I MIGHT SAVE SOME MONEY FOR ONCE!

I'M LOOKING AT ALL THESE FASHIONS THROUGH THE DECADES...
I COULD GO AS A 20'S INSPIRED FLAPPER...
Style through the DECADES
THE THIRTIES WERE GLAMOROUS, TOO...
AND THE FORTIES HAD THAT DAZZLING MOVIE STAR STYLE...

MAYBE I COULD GO FOR A "MARILYN MONROE" LOOK FROM THE 50'S!
YOU'RE MORE OF THE "ELIZABETH TAYLOR" STYLE!
HOW ABOUT THAT MOD SIXTIES LOOK?
AND THINGS GOT REAL PSYCHADELIC LATER ON!
3

THE SEVENTIES STYLES ARE THE COOLEST!
WOW! THESE ARE A LOT LIKE THE FASHIONS OF TODAY!
WHAT ABOUT THE EIGHTIES?
NOT BAD! BUT I REALLY LIKE THE SEVENTIES STYLES BEST!
4

I HEAR YOU GIRLS!
YOU LIKE SEVENTIES FASHIONS TOO, MOM?
I CERTAINLY DO!
THAT'S WHEN I WENT TO MY PROM!
PHOTOS
HERE'S ME IN MY PROM DRESS!
OHMIGOSH!
THAT DRESS IS AWESOME!
THAT'S IT! THAT'S THE DRESS I WANT!
I CAN TRY AND MAKE IT FOR YOU!
NO NEED FOR THAT!
COME WITH ME!

I STILL HAVE IT IN STORAGE!
WOW!
LOOK! IT FITS BEAUTIFULLY!
I'VE GOT TO SHOW DADDY!
DADDY! LOOK AT MY PROM DRESS!
UH-OH! HOW MUCH IS THIS GOING TO COST ME?
NOTHING!
IT'S MOM'S OLD PROM DRESS! IT'S FREE!
FWOMP!!
SOON...
I-I HAD THIS CRAZY DREAM! FOR ONCE, VERONICA DIDN'T COST ME ANY MONEY...
end

WILL BETTY & VERONICA FIND THE CURE FOR...
PROM-ITIS?
YOU'RE GOING TO THE PROM WITH WHO?!
SHULTZ
KOSLOWSKI

FOR THOSE OF YOU WHO DON'T KNOW ME, ALLOW ME TO INTRODUCE MYSELF...
MY NAME IS MR. WEATHERBEE, AND I'M PRINCIPAL OF THIS FINE ESTABLISH-MENT, RIVERDALE HIGH SCHOOL!
I'VE BEEN PRINCIPAL FOR OVER--
WELL--
LET'S JUST SAY IT'S BEEN A VERY LONG TIME!
FOR THE MOST PART, RIVERDALE HIGH IS A PROGRESSIVE HIGH SCHOOL WITH POLITE, CARING, INTELLIGENT TEENAGERS!
AFTER YOU.
THANKS.
THAT IS, UNTIL THIS TIME OF YEAR WHEN PRACTICALLY EVERY STUDENT CATCHES A DREADED DISEASE!

Betty and Veronica in A CASE OF PROM-ITIS
PROMITIS IS VERY CONTAGIOUS. ONE OF THE SYMPTOMS SEEN IN OUR FEMALE POPULATION IS THAT THEY TALK ABOUT NOTHING BUT FASHION.
I SAW THE MOST AWESOME DRESS AT LACY'S. IT'S PURPLE, WITH TINY T-STRAPS, ABOUT FIVE ROWS OF RUFFLES...
WOW! IT SOUNDS AMAZING, MIDGE! ARE YOU GOING TO WEAR IT TO THE PROM?
MOST LIKELY! BUT I'M GOING TO HAVE ANOTHER LOOK AT IT AFTER SCHOOL. WANNA COME?
SURE! THAT SOUNDS LIKE FUN!
JUST TWO MORE ALL-NIGHTERS AND I SHOULD HAVE MY PROM GOWN ALL SEWN UP!
WOW, BETTY! I REALLY ADMIRE YOU FOR MAKING YOUR OWN DRESS!
DADDYKINS SENT HIS PRIVATE JET TO PARIS TO PICK UP PIERRE VON VASHION FOR MY FINAL FITTING. HE'S DESIGNED AN EXCLUSIVE GOWN JUST FOR ME!
WOW! THAT'S AWESOME!! VERONICA LODGE, YOU ARE SO LUCKY TO BE YOU!
MY DRESS IS GOLD WITH SILVER STARS!
MINE IS BROWN WITH PINK POLKA DOTS!
2

"PROMITIS ALSO AFFECTS THE MALE POPULATION... REGGIE MANTLE'S EGO IS EVEN BIGGER THAN EVER!
GIRLS, GIRLS, GIRLS! JUST BECAUSE YOU AREN'T PROM MATERIAL DOESN'T MEAN YOU'RE NOT ALL BEAUTIFUL!
IT'S JUST THAT I HAVE ONLY SO MANY DANCE CARDS TO GIVE OUT!
I WANT ONE!
MOVE!
HEY!
"AND DILTON DOILEY HASN'T LOOKED IN HIS MATH BOOK IN A WEEK!"
I'VE BEEN CALCULATING MY DANCE EQUATIONS SO I WON'T TRIP AT THE PROM OR STEP ON ANYONE'S TOES!
WOW, DILTON! YOU'RE SO INSPIRING!
AND A-ONE, AND A-TWO AND RIGHT HALF STEP OVER LEFT CIRCLE 180 DEGREES AND A--
BUT I THINK ARCHIE ANDREWS MAY HAVE THE WORST CASE OF PROMITIS YET! HE'S BEEN HIDING OUT ALL WEEK!
"DO I INVITE BETTY...
...OR VERONICA?"

ARCHIE'S PROMITIS IS SO ADVANCED THAT HIS GRADES HAVE DROPPED EVEN LOWER THAN THEY WERE BEFORE!
ARCHIE ANDREWS D- MATH D+ SCIEN D- HISTO D ENGLI
"I TRIED TALKING SOME SENSE TO THE LAD...
I REALIZE THESE ARE STRESSFUL TIMES, BUT YOU NEED TO BUCKLE DOWN AND PULL UP YOUR GRADES! YOUR FUTURE IS AT STAKE!
DO YOU UNDERSTAND WHAT I'M SAYING TO YOU, ARCHIE?
YES, SIR.
THAT'S GOOD! I'M GLAD WE HAD THIS LITTLE TALK, LAD!
ME TOO, SIR.
ANY QUESTIONS?
YES, MR. WEATHER-BEE...
...WHO DO YOU THINK I SHOULD INVITE TO THE PROM? BETTY OR VERONICA?
"...BUT IT WAS HOPELESS!"

"AND THEN THERE'S DEAR, SWEET BETTY COOPER, WHO IS NORMALLY A SENSIBLE, STRAIGHT A STUDENT.
THE ANSWER IS FIVE SQUARED!
CORRECT!
"SHE'S EDITOR-IN-CHIEF OF OUR FINE SCHOOL PAPER!"
WHO'S GOT THE LEAD STORY?
I DO!
I DO!
OUT
AND SHE'S RECEIVED THE DISTINGUISHED HONOR OF BEING NAMED "THE GOOD CITIZEN OF RIVERDALE"!
CONGRATULATIONS, BETTY. JOB WELL DONE.
THANK YOU, MR. WEATHERBEE.
GO, BETTY!
WE'RE PROUD OF YOU!
BRAVO!
BUT LOOK AT HER NOW!
YAWN!
SHE CAN BARELY KEEP HER EYES OPEN FROM PROMITIS!
I JUST HAVE 500 MORE SEQUINS TO SEW ON MY DRESS!

PROMITIS IS SPREADING FASTER THAN ETHEL CHASING JUGHEAD!
AND MORE SERIOUS THAN NANCY BREAKING UP WITH CHUCK!
BUT--BUT! THE PROM IS THE SAME NIGHT AS THE BIG COMIC BOOK CONVENTION!
IT'S EITHER ME OR YOUR COMICS!
"AND THE PROM COMMITTEE IS GOING FOR BROKE!"
WE SHOULD HAVE THE PROM AT THE RIVER-DALE COUNTRY CLUB!
THE GYM IS TACKY, TACKY, TACKY!
BUT IT'S SO EXPENSIVE!
I'D HAVE TO WORK DOUBLE SHIFTS JUST TO PAY FOR MY TICKET!
IT'S OUR PROM!
MONEY IS NO OBJECT!

MR. WEATHERBEE, HAVE YOU SEEN ARCHIE?
WE'RE LOOKING EVERYWHERE FOR HIM!
HMM... I THINK HE WENT THAT WAY!
PHEW! THANKS, SIR!
SOMETIMES WE MEN HAVE TO STICK TOGETHER, ARCHIE!
IT'S MY TURN! YOU WENT TO SPRING FLING WITH HIM!
BUT YOU HAD HIM ALL THROUGH THE HOLIDAYS WHEN I WENT SKIING IN SWITZERLAND!
BELIEVE IT OR NOT, THOSE GIRLS ARE NORMALLY BEST FRIENDS!

NOW I'M NOT SAYING THAT I MYSELF AM COMPLETELY IMMUNE TO PROMITIS!
WHY, BACK IN THE DAY, MISS GRUNDY AND I--
--WELL, THAT'S ANOTHER STORY...!
BUT THIS YEAR'S CASE OF PROMITIS IS ABSOLUTELY THE WORST I'VE SEEN IN ALL MY YEARS AS PRINCIPAL OF THESE HALLOWED HALLS!
SIGH
I'M AFRAID THERE'S ONLY ONE THING I CAN DO. BUT FIRST I HAVE TO RUN IT BY MY FACULTY...

LATER THAT DAY...
I VINISHED ZE DRESS FOR YOU, MISS VERONICA!
NOW CLOSE YOUR EYES!
NOW-- OPEN!
IT'S THE MOST BEAUTIFUL GOWN IN THE WORLD!
BUT IT'S SO UNFAIR!
"WHEN I MAKE MY GRAND ENTRANCE, NONE OF THE OTHER GIRLS WILL BE ABLE TO COMPETE!"
LOOK AT VERONICA!
SHE'S BREATH-TAKING!
HOW WILL WE EVER COM-PETE?!

"BUT THERE'S SOMETHING WRONG WITH THIS PICTURE...
"AND IT'S ARCHIE! HE TAKES AWAY FROM THE GLORIOUSNESS OF ME!
MEANWHILE, AT LACY'S...
WHAT DO YOU THINK, NANCY?
IT'S PRETTY, BUT THE COLOR IS NOT YOU, MIDGE!
A HALF AN HOUR LATER...
HOW DO YOU LIKE THIS ONE, MIDGE?
SO LAST YEAR!
TWO HOURS LATER...
WELL?
NO. WELL?
NO.
10

I'LL NEVER BE ABLE TO FIND THE RIGHT DRESS.!
JUST 12 MORE TO TRY ON.!!
AND I'LL NEVER BE ABLE TO GET HOME.!

THIS IS IT!
FINALLY!
HEY!
oh, NO!
THAT'S MY DRESS!

I DECIDED TO GO TO THE PROM WITH NANCY INSTEAD OF THE COMIC CONVENTION, ARCHIE!
ED's TUXEDO SHOP
GOOD DECISION, CHUCK.
I SURE HOPE SHE LIKES THE TUXEDO I CHOSE.
I THINK BETTY WILL LIKE THIS ONE...
13
...BUT ON THE OTHER HAND, VERONICA WOULD PROBABLY LIKE THAT ONE!
13
IF I ONLY KNEW WHICH GIRL TO INVITE TO THE PROM-- THEN I'D KNOW WHICH TUXEDO TO RENT!
AT BETTY COOPER'S HOUSE...
BETTY, DEAR! IT'S PAST MIDNIGHT! YOU NEED TO GET YOUR REST!
THIS PROM DRESS HAS TAKEN OVER YOUR LIFE!
I JUST HAVE A COUPLE OF HUNDRED MORE SEQUINS TO SEW ON AND I'LL BE ALL FINISHED!

BACK AT RIVERDALE HIGH...
I HATE TO SAY IT, WALDO, BUT I MUST AGREE WITH YOU.
I SECOND THAT!
I THIRD IT!

THEN IT'S *OFFICIAL*. I'LL MAKE THE ANNOUNCEMENT FIRST THING IN THE MORNING!

THIS MEETING IS *ADJOURNED*.
RIVERDALE H.S.

THE NEXT MORNING...
ATTENTION ALL STUDENTS! I HAVE AN IMPORTANT ANNOUNCE-MENT TO MAKE! THERE WILL BE NO PROM THIS YEAR!
N-NO PROM?!
DID HE JUST SAY NO PROM?
WHAT?!
I JUST HEARD MR. WEATHERBEE SAY THERE WAS NO PROM! I MUST BE DREAMING!
IF YOU WERE DREAMING, BETTY, THEN I JUST HAD THE SAME NIGHT-MARE!
BUT I JUST LEARNED THE HOKEY POKEY!
I FINALLY GOT ALL MY GIRLS LINED UP!

...AND IT'S RED AT THE BOTTOM AND LIGHT RED AT THE TOP, BUT IT ACTUALLY IS MORE LIKE A PINK...
GASP!
I KNOW, RIGHT? IT'LL BE PERFECT FOR MY GRAND ENTRANCE!
?
NO PROM? BUT I WAS JUST ABOUT TO CHOOSE...
ARCHIEKINS! THERE YOU ARE! I'VE BEEN LOOKING FOR YOU EVERYWHERE!
I KNOW YOU HAD YOUR HEART SET ON GOING TO THE PROM WITH ME... BUT I'VE DECIDED TO DO MY ENTRANCE SOLO!
BUT... BUT, VERONICA...
PLEASE, ARCHIE! DON'T MAKE THIS MORE DIFFICULT THAN IT HAS TO BE.
I CAN'T BELIEVE THE BEE CANCELLED THE PROM!
ME EITHER!
YOU CAN ALWAYS TAKE BETTY.
DOESN'T SHE KNOW THERE IS NO PROM?

IT'S NOT FAIR!
WE'VE BEEN LOOKING FORWARD TO THE PROM ALL YEAR!
WE DESERVE OUR PROM!
THE PROM IS A TRADITION!
IT'S OUR RIGHT!
STOMP
LET'S ALL MEET AT POP'S AFTER SCHOOL! THE BEE CAN'T DO THIS TO US!
MEET AT POP'S AFTER SCHOOL.
MEET AT POP'S AFTER SCHOOL!
MEET AT POP'S AFTER SCHOOL!
I CAN'T POSSIBLY!
I HAVE MY FINAL FITTING TONIGHT!
MEET AT--
Oh, NEVER MIND!
?

A GOOD REPORTER IS OBJECTIVE!
A GOOD REPORTER REPORTS THE FACTS!
A GOOD REPORTER STAYS COOL!
NOK NOK
PRINCIPAL
IT'S ME, MR. WEATHERBEE. I WAS WONDERING IF I COULD INTERVIEW YOU FOR THE SCHOOL PAPER...
WHY, OF COURSE, BETTY. COME RIGHT IN.
HOW COULD YOU CANCEL OUR PROM?!
THAT'S A VERY GOOD QUESTION, BETTY. ONE WHICH I REALLY THOUGHT LONG AND HARD ABOUT!
NORMALLY, I'M PROUD TO BE PRINCIPAL OF THIS FINE ESTABLISHMENT. RIVERDALE IS A PROGRESSIVE SCHOOL WITH POLITE, CARING AND INTELLIGENT STUDENTS...

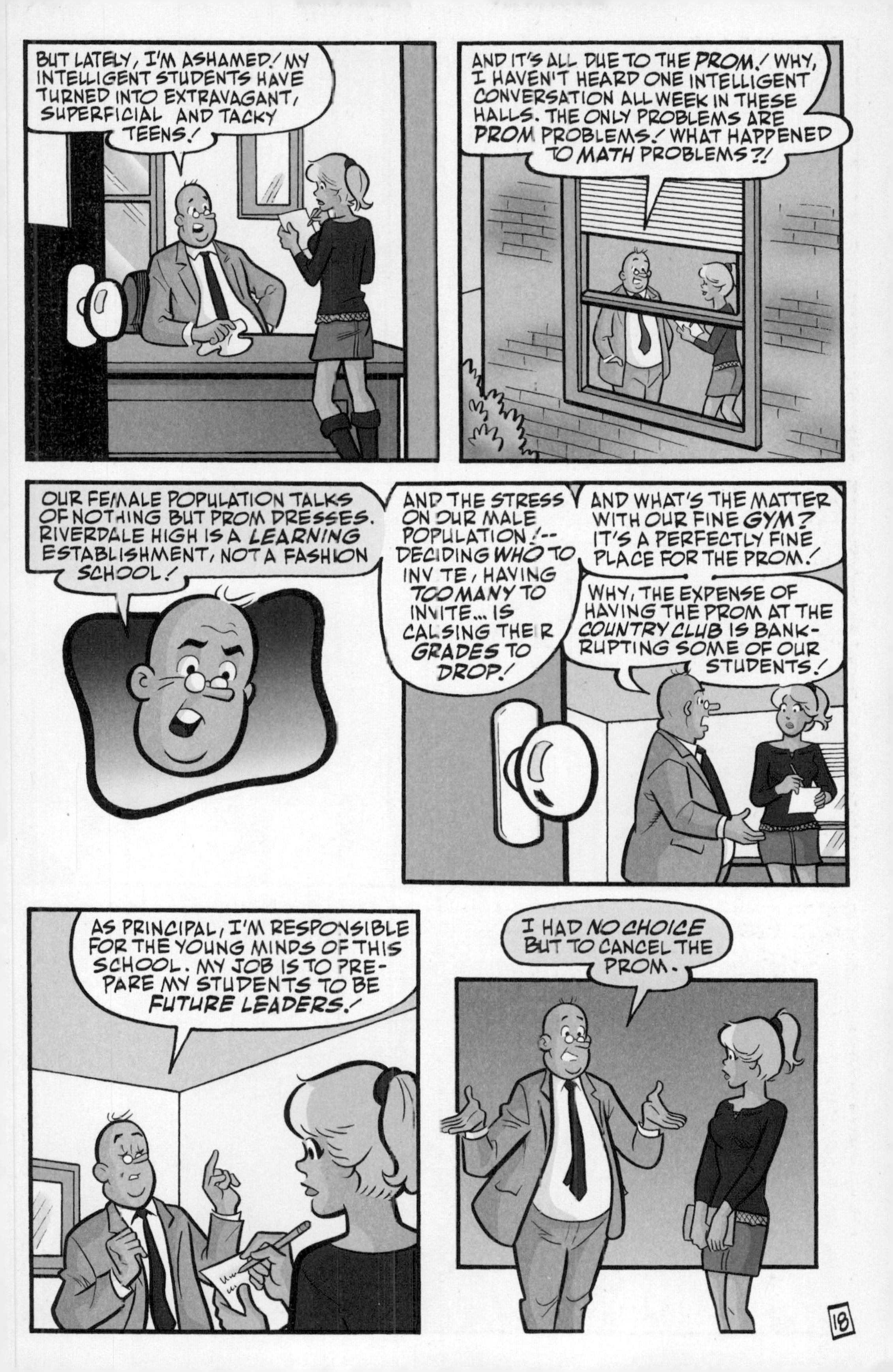
BUT LATELY, I'M ASHAMED! MY INTELLIGENT STUDENTS HAVE TURNED INTO EXTRAVAGANT, SUPERFICIAL AND TACKY TEENS!
AND IT'S ALL DUE TO THE PROM! WHY, I HAVEN'T HEARD ONE INTELLIGENT CONVERSATION ALL WEEK IN THESE HALLS. THE ONLY PROBLEMS ARE PROM PROBLEMS! WHAT HAPPENED TO MATH PROBLEMS?!
OUR FEMALE POPULATION TALKS OF NOTHING BUT PROM DRESSES. RIVERDALE HIGH IS A LEARNING ESTABLISHMENT, NOT A FASHION SCHOOL!
AND THE STRESS ON OUR MALE POPULATION!-- DECIDING WHO TO INVITE, HAVING TOO MANY TO INVITE... IS CAUSING THEIR GRADES TO DROP!
AND WHAT'S THE MATTER WITH OUR FINE GYM? IT'S A PERFECTLY FINE PLACE FOR THE PROM!
WHY, THE EXPENSE OF HAVING THE PROM AT THE COUNTRY CLUB IS BANKRUPTING SOME OF OUR STUDENTS!
AS PRINCIPAL, I'M RESPONSIBLE FOR THE YOUNG MINDS OF THIS SCHOOL. MY JOB IS TO PREPARE MY STUDENTS TO BE FUTURE LEADERS!
I HAD NO CHOICE BUT TO CANCEL THE PROM.
18

AT POP'S...
WHAT DO WE WANT?
PROM!
WE WANT OUR PROM
WHEN DO WE WANT IT?
NOW!
EXTRA! EXTRA! READ ALL ABOUT IT! EXCLUSIVE INTERVIEW WITH THE BEE!
LET ME READ THAT!
LET'S SEE WHAT OL' SCROOGE HAS TO SAY FOR HIMSELF!
YEAH! HOW COULD HE DEFEND HIMSELF?
"OUR FEMALE POPULATION TALKS NOTHING BUT FASHION.
GEE...THAT SOUNDS LIKE ME! I HOPE I WASN'T RESPONSIBLE FOR THE PROM BEING CANCELLED!
"AND WHAT'S THE MATTER WITH OUR FINE GYM? IT'S THE PERFECT PLACE FOR A PROM!
I WONDER IF MY INSISTING IT BE AT THE CLUB MADE THE BEE CANCEL THE PROM?
"AND THE STRESS ON OUR MALE POPULATION HAS CAUSED GRADES TO DROP."
GEE, MR. WEATHERBEE DID TRY TO TALK SOME SENSE TO ME... BUT I JUST WASN'T LISTENING!

NEXT MORNING...
WHAT'S THIS ALL ABOUT?
PRINCIPAL
MR. WEATHERBEE, WE'RE SORRY WE WERE FIGHTING OVER OUR FASHIONS!
IF YOU NEED TO PUNISH ANYONE, PUNISH US; BUT PLEASE LET THE PROM GO ON!
MR. WEATHERBEE, I AGREE THAT THE GYM IS A SUITABLE PLACE FOR THE PROM. AND I PROMISE TO CUT BACK ON MY GIRLS AND ONLY CHOOSE THREE!
MR. WEATHERBEE, I PROMISE TO STUDY AND PULL UP MY GRADES!
I'M SORRY I DIDN'T LISTEN TO YOU.
MR. WEATHERBEE, I'LL GET BACK TO MATH PROBLEMS INSTEAD OF DANCE STEPS! I DIDN'T LIKE THE HOKEY POKEY ANYWAY!
AND I'LL NEVER STAY UP ALL NIGHT AND NEGLECT MY STUDIES FOR A SILLY DRESS AGAIN!

Hmm... MY STUDENTS SEEM TO HAVE LEARNED THEIR LESSONS.
PERHAPS I WAS A BIT HASTY IN CANCELLING THE--
--PROM?
MERCY BE! THAT'S A PICTURE OF MISS GRUNDY AND ME!
Oh, DEAR! I DO BELIEVE I'VE CAUGHT A MILD CASE OF PROMITIS MYSELF!
ATTENTION ALL STUDENTS! I HAVE AN IMPORTANT ANNOUNCEMENT TO MAKE! THERE WILL BE A PROM AFTER ALL!! IT WILL BE HELD IN THE GYMNASIUM!
YEAH!
THE BEE'S OKAY BY ME!
HIP, HIP, HOORAY!
MEANWHILE...
GOODBYE, PIERRE VON VASHION!
DADDYKINS, WILL YOU DROP ME OFF AT SCHOOL? I'M A LITTLE LATE BECAUSE I SIMPLY HAD TO SAY GOODBYE TO PIERRE!
OF COURSE, PRINCESS!

DAYS LATER, AT THE PROM...
I LOVE YOUR TUXEDO, CHUCK.
THANKS, NANCY!
YOU LOOK BEAUTIFUL, MIDGE!
BUT ISN'T YOUR DRESS THE SAME AS NANCY'S?
Oh, YES! WE DECIDED THAT IT LOOKED GREAT ON BOTH OF US.
I'M HAVING A GREAT TIME, ARCHIE!
ME TOO, BETTY!
BUT I WONDER WHERE VERONICA IS!
I'M SO GLAD WE'RE HAVING THE PROM IN THE GYM!
ME TOO!
ME THREE!
GIRLS, GIRLS, GIRLS! YOU'RE THE CHOSEN THREE!
DO YOU WANNA DANCE, JUGGIE?
AS SOON AS I FINISH EATING!
MAY I HAVE THIS DANCE, MISS GRUNDY?
WHY CERTAINLY, WALDO.

MEANWHILE...
MAKE-UP? CHECK.
DRESS? CHECK.
MY TOTALLY GORGEOUS SELF?
DEFINITELY CHECK!
WELL... THIS IS IT...
TA-DAH!
I'M HERE!
HEY--WHERE IS EVERYBODY?!
DON'T YOU KNOW? THE RIVERDALE PROM WAS MOVED TO THE GYM!
WHAT?!
BUT YOU DO LOOK LOVELY, MISS VERONICA!
END

YOUR PROM OR MINE?!
THE GREAT THING ABOUT *PROM TIME* THIS YEAR...
...LOTS OF *NEW KIDS* TO CHOOSE FROM!
Dan Parent

Betty and Veronica
IN
YOUR PROM OR MINE?!
VERY NICE, RON! THAT'S THE PRETTIEST ONE YET!
THANKS, BETTY! I AGREE!
HAVE WE NARROWED IT DOWN YET, MISS LODGE?
1

YES! I'VE NARROWED IT DOWN TO THESE TWELVE!
I GUESS I'LL JUST TAKE THEM ALL!
KA-CHING
I CAN DECIDE WHAT TO WEAR THAT DAY!
WHAT A LUXURY!
AND YOU, MISS COOPER?
I'LL TAKE THIS ONE!
IT'S LOVELY, BETTY!
AND IT'S 75% OFF, SO THAT MAKES MY DECISION EASY!
LOOK, JUG! IT'S THAT TIME OF YEAR!
WHAT? TO PLANT YOUR SPRING GARDEN?
Lee's
DRESS BOUTIQUE
2

NO! IT'S PROM SEASON!
LOOKS LIKE THE GIRLS ARE GETTING READY!
I THINK I PREFER FLU SEASON!
I WONDER WHO I'LL ASK!
WHO DID I TAKE TO THE LAST BIG DANCE?
WAS IT BETTY...? OR WAS IT VERONICA?
DOES IT MAKE A DIFFERENCE?
HI, GIRLS! PREPPING FOR THE PROM?
MAYBE!
I'M JUST TRYING TO FIGURE OUT WHO TO ASK THIS YEAR!
WELL, YOU WENT WITH VERONICA LAST DANCE...
SO I GUESS IT'S MY TURN!

WAITAMINUTE!! YOU WENT TO THE CHRISTMAS BALL TOGETHER...
SO IT SHOULD BE MY TURN FOR THE NEXT BIG EVENT!
AH, DARN!
I WANTED TO TAKE YOU BOTH TO THE PROM!
HAHAHA!!
YOU SHOULD SEE THE GOOFY LOOKS ON YOUR FACES!
I'D SOONER GO TO THE PROM WITH A TREE STUMP!
WELL, I HAVE ONE WORD FOR THAT TREE STUMP...
RUN!!
I'LL SORT THIS ALL OUT LATER... I HAVE A BASKET-BALL GAME TO GET TO!
4

I'M HUNGRY! LET'S GRAB SOME LUNCH!
I COULD USE A BURGER FROM POP'S!
WHAT ARE YOU LOOKING FOR?
JUGHEAD!
I WANT TO MAKE SURE HIS FREELOADING EARS DIDN'T HEAR THAT!

SOON!!
Oh, LOOK--IT'S SAYID!
HI, SAYID!

WOW! I MUST SAY, HE'S ONE OF THE CUTER NEW KIDS!
uh, BETTY... CAN I HAVE A QUICK WORD WITH YOU?

Hmm... WHAT ARE THEY WHISPERING ABOUT?

HE LOOKS LIKE HE HAS A THING FOR BETTY!
AND SHE'S NOT EXACTLY FIGHTING HIM OFF!
I'LL ANXIOUSLY AWAIT YOUR ANSWER!
OKAY, SAYID!
HE ASKED ME TO THE PROM!
WHAT?! WHAT DID YOU SAY?
I TOLD HIM I WAS WAITING ON ARCHIE!
POP'S
Oh, I SEE...
HE'S A CUTIE! YOU SHOULD GO...
AND HAND ARCHIE OVER TO YOU ON A SILVER PLATTER?...
NO THANK YOU!

WHO COULD THAT BE?
OH, IT'S ROB MONTAUKETT!
RING!
HOW'D HE GET MY NUMBER?
NOT THAT I MIND... HE'S HOT!
POP'S
OOPS! YOU HEARD THAT? SORRY!
YOU WANT TO ASK ME SOME-THING?
OKAY...
YOU WANT TO ASK ME TO THE PROM?
WELL, UH... LET ME GET BACK TO YOU...
POP'S
HE ASKED YOU TO THE PROM?
HOW EXCITING!
BETTY! WE'VE BEEN FOOLS!
DO YOU REALIZE JUST HOW MUCH WE'RE LIMITING OURSELVES?
7

THERE'S A WHOLE MENU OF NEW DISHES OUT THERE!
AND WE'RE LIMITING OURSELVES TO THE SAME BORING ENTRÉE!
I TAKE IT YOU'RE NOT TALKING ABOUT FOOD!
NO! WE'VE HAD AN INFLUX OF NEW STUDENTS AT RIVERDALE HIGH!
MANY OF THEM HUNKS!
HELLO, GIRLS.
WELL, AND A FEW EXCEPTIONS!
BUT REGARDLESS, WE SHOULD BE EXPLORING NEW HORIZONS!
I THINK WE SHOULD GO WITH ONE OF THE NEW KIDS TO THE PROM!
I DON'T KNOW, RON...

I'M KIND OF OLD SCHOOL...
YOO-HOO! HI, GIRLS!
Oh, HI, SHEILA! HI, CHLOE!
DID YOU HEAR THE NEWS? I'M GOING TO THE PROM WITH ARCHIE!
AND I'M GOING WITH JUGHEAD!
WHAT?!
H-HOW? WE JUST SAW THEM!!
WHEN DID THEY ASK YOU?
WE ASKED THEM!
WE BELIEVE IN TAKING THE BULL BY THE HORNS!
AND HOW DID YOU GET JUGHEAD TO GO TO THE PROM AT ALL?
I TOLD HIM ABOUT MY AUNTIE'S ITALIAN RESTAURANT! IT'S AN ALL-YOU-CAN-EAT BUFFET!
9

HOW DO YOU LIKE THAT?
THEY'RE RIGHT!
WHAT?
WE NEED TO DO EXACTLY WHAT THEY DID!
TAKE THE BULL BY THE HORNS!!
I'M GOING TO GET THE PHONE NUMBERS OF ALL THE NEW KIDS!
THE NEW GUYS, THAT IS!
WHAT'S SHE COOKING UP?
DO I EVEN WANT TO KNOW?
A FEW DAYS LATER!
VERONICA, WHAT'S GOING ON? I FEEL ONE OF YOUR CRAZY SCHEMES AT WORK!
YOU MEAN "CLEVER SCHEMES"!
POP'S

B&V'S PROM TRYOUTS?
WHAT?!
PLEASE EXPLAIN!
B&V's PROM TRYOUTS TODAY!
IT'S SIMPLE!
YOU'VE HEARD OF SPEED DATING, RIGHT?
YOU MEAN, WHERE YOU HAVE A FEW MINUTES TO MEET SOMEONE?
THEN YOU MOVE ON TO THE NEXT DATE...
POP'
B&V's PROM TRYOUTS TODA
AT THE END OF THE SESSION, YOU PICK YOUR FAVORITE..
AND WHO'S COMING TO THIS EVENT?
WELL, I INVITED EVERY NEW GUY IN SCHOOL...
WHAT IF NOBODY SHOWS UP?
I DON'T THINK THAT'LL BE A PROBLEM!!
11

I CAN'T BELIEVE POP *AGREED* TO THIS!
ARE YOU *KIDDING*?! T'S TONS OF NEW *BUSINESS* FOR HIM!
AND LOOK AT THE *TURNOUT*!
WE'RE BETTY AND VERONICA! *EVERYBODY* WANTS TO DATE US!
12
OKAY--LET'S *START*! THERE'S 5 MINUTES FOR EACH BOY!
GO!

WHY SHOULD I GO TO THE PROM WITH YOU, ROB?
BECAUSE... I'M HOT!
WORKS FOR ME!
UH... WHY DO YOU WANT TO BE MY PROM DATE, SIMON?
BECAUSE MY MOM SAYS I SHOULD GET OUT OF THE HOUSE!
YOU SWEET-TALKER!
OKAY, VIC! WHY ME?
BECAUSE YOU'RE THE LOVELIEST GIRL IN THE WORLD!
KISS!
WELL, I CAN'T ARGUE WITH THAT!
THIS IS KIND OF SILLY!
I SUPPOSE! BUT IF THIS IS WHAT IT TAKES, IT'S WORTH IT!
13

I REALLY LIKE YOU, BETTY!
I LIKE YOU, TOO, SAYID!
WHY SHOULD I GIVE YOU THE HONOR OF GOING TO THE PROM WITH ME?
WHAT?!! IT'S THE OTHER WAY AROUND, BUDDY!!
YOU SEEM LIKE TOO MUCH WORK! I DON'T THINK THIS'LL WORK OUT!
SORRY TO WASTE YOUR TIME!
Hmmm... NOT BAD!
Oh, HE'S A REAL FIRECRACKER!
HI, CHUNK!
AREN'T YOU GOING SAY SOMETHING?
14

I'M KINDA FREAKED OUT...
WHO'S YOUR DADDY?
SO, LAWRENCE, YOU'RE FILTHY RICH, LIKE ME!
Ahem!
I'M RICHER THAN YOU!
NEXT!!
SOON!
THANK YOU ALL FOR SHOWING UP!
AFTER TABULATING YOUR SCORES...
I WILL BE ATTENDING THE PROM WITH SAYID!
AND I WILL BE ATTENDING THE PROM WITH SAYID!
WHAT?!
I'M NOT COMPLAINING!
Oh, NO!! WHAT IS IT WITH US?!!

OKAY! OKAY! HE ALREADY ASKED YOU, SO YOU WIN THAT ONE!
I'LL GO WITH THE GUY WHO SCORED NEXT HIGHEST...
DANNY! IT LOOKS LIKE IT'S YOU AND ME!
REALLY? I MUST SAY I'M KIND OF SURPRISED!
I LIKE A CHALLENGE!
THEN YOU PICKED THE RIGHT GUY, SWEETIE!
AND DON'T WORRY, ALL YOU REJECTED ONES...
WHO'S YOUR DADDY
ALL OUR OTHER FRIENDS ARE WAITING IN THE WINGS!
ISN'T ANYBODY GOING TO EAT?!
Menu

PROM NIGHT!
Oh, SAYID! YOU LOOK SO HANDSOME!
NOT NEARLY AS MAGNIFI-CENT AS YOU!!
WHAT ARE YOU WEARING?! IS--IS THAT A TUXEDO T-SHIRT?!
HEY, HOT STUFF!
THAT'S RIGHT!
DID YOU GET YOUR FASHION TIPS FROM JUGHEAD!?!
WHAT A LOVELY LIMO!
THERE'S JUST ONE LITTLE THING...
I HAVE TO BRING MY SIBLINGS!
MY PARENTS ARE AWAY AND OUR BABYSITTER IS SICK!
Oh, THAT'S PRETTY!
HEY! I WANNA SEE!
POP

WHAT IS THAT?!
THAT'S MY BIKE! I CLEANED IT UP JUST FOR YOU!
IF THAT'S CLEAN, I'D HATE TO SEE IT DIRTY!
HOW AM I GOING TO RIDE ON THAT?
I BROUGHT A HELMET FOR YOU!
OF COURSE, IF YOU'RE TOO CHICKEN...
I KNEW YOU'D BE A CHALLENGE... LET'S JUST DO THIS!
VVRR-ROAR
SO
THERE'S ARCHIE AND SHEILA!
Oh, LOOK! GINGER CAME WITH LONNIE!
AND SIMON CAME WITH ETHEL!
HOW CUTE!
18

BOBBI AND REGGIE!
THAT SHOULD BE AN INTERESTING PAIR!
YOU'RE HERE, RON!
BARELY! MY HAIR'S A MESS FROM THIS HELMET!!
AND THERE'S MOTOR OIL ON MY DRESS!
Oh, THE NEXT SONG IS STARTING!
I LOVE THIS SONG!
LET'S DANCE!
US FIRST!!
HMPH!!
WANNA DANCE?
NAH! I HATE POP MUSIC! I'LL WAIT FOR SOME ROCK!
YOU'RE TOO MUCH!
19

THERE'S VIC! HE LOOKS ALONE!
VIC, DO YOU WANT TO DANCE?
OKAY! BUT I'M NOT VERY GOOD COMPANY.
I'LL BE THE JUDGE OF THAT!
SOON...
Oh, I LOVE THIS BALLAD!
DANCE WITH ME AGAIN!
MY "DATE" IS STILL BABY-SITTING!!
OKAY!
SOB!
VIC! WHAT'S WRONG?
IT'S JUST... I MISS MY GIRL!
WHEN WE TRANSFERRED FROM PINE POINT, SHE WENT TO THE LANDVIEW SCHOOL DISTRICT!
20

I DON'T SEE HER ANYMORE!
SHE THOUGHT IT WAS BEST TO MOVE ON!
BUT I'M HAVING A HARD TIME...!
WHY, YOU BIG ROMANTIC LUG!
VIC, I'M HERE FOR YOU IF YOU NEED A FRIEND TO TALK TO...
THANKS, BETTY! YOU KNOW, IT'S HARD TO TALK ABOUT THIS... ESPECIALLY WITH MY BUDDIES...
HEY--BETTY!! Oh--IT LOOKS LIKE SHE'S MADE A NEW FRIEND!
C'MON, SAYID! I LOVE THIS SONG!
ARCHIE! WHERE'S SHEILA?
DANCING WITH ALL HER ADMIRERS!
21

SHE ACTS LIKE THIS IS A NIGHT-CLUB!
AT LEAST YOUR DATE LIKES TO DANCE!
MINE'S ALREADY DISSED ME FOR HIS FRIENDS!
WHAT'S YOUR STORY, BETTY?
WELL, MY DATE'S BABYSITTING!
AND I'M COUNSELING ON THE SIDE!
NOT MY IDEA OF AN EXCITING PROM!
WELL, GIRLS... MAY I HAVE THIS DANCE?
YES!!
ISN'T IT FUNNY?
NO MATTER WHO OR WHAT ENTERS OUR LIVES...

IT ALWAYS BOILS DOWN TO THE THREE OF US!
PRETTY PATHETIC, HUH?
OOOH! ARCHIE, THEY'RE PLAYING OUR SONG!
SINCE WHEN IS THAT YOUR SONG?
YOU CAN HAVE THE NEXT DANCE!
WHO MADE YOU QUEEN OF THE PROM?!
THIS PROM'S KIND OF MESSED UP!
YEAH! I WONDER IF ANYONE'S HAVING A GOOD NIGHT!
THIS IS THE BEST PROM NIGHT EVER!
WE HAVEN'T EVEN LEFT YET! YOU'VE BEEN PIGGING OUT IN OUR RESTAURANT ALL NIGHT!
I'LL BE READY TO LEAVE IN A LITTLE WHILE... JUST ONE MORE TRAY OF LASAGNA, PLEASE!
END

Prom Showdown!
UH-OH! THIS ISN'T GOING TO BE PRETTY!
Dan Parent

Veronica in Prom SHOWDOWN!
OH, THAT'S RIGHT! I ALMOST FORGOT! THE PROM IS COMING UP!
I'VE GOT TO ASK ARCHIE BEFORE BETTY GETS TO HIM FIRST!
Spring Prom
HA HA
Ah, THERE HE IS, RIPE FOR THE PICKING!
ARCHIE, I HAVE SOMETHING I NEED TO ASK YOU...

BETTY! WHAT ARE YOU DOING? I NEED TO ASK ARCHIE SOMETHING!
AND LOOK AT WHAT THE CAT DRAGGED IN!
VERY FUNNY.
ARCHIE, I WANT TO ASK YOU...
WILL YOU GO TO THE PROM WITH ME?!!
YOU'VE GOT TO BE KIDDING!
TALK ABOUT BAD TIMING!
OKAY, ARCHIE! WHO WILL IT BE? MAKE A DECISION!

I DON'T THINK I CAN!
SO, I'LL TAKE ALL THREE OF YOU!
WHATZ!
I'LL DANCE AND HANG OUT WITH ALL THREE OF YOU! PROBLEM SOLVED!
OH, GREAT.
WELL, IT'S ONLY FAIR, I GUESS.
I'M GOING TO HAVE TO GET THE DRESS OF A LIFETIME TO OUTSHINE THESE TWO!
ANY IDEA WHAT YOU'RE GOING TO WEAR?
OH, JUST ONE OF THE MANY GOWNS IN MY CLOSET.
THIS IS A FASHION CODE RED!
MOM, I NEED A SUPER-EXPENSIVE, FABULOUS DESIGNER DRESS FOR THE PROM!

FINE!
YOU HAVE PLENTY UP IN YOUR CLOSET!
THOSE ARE SO LAST YEAR!
I NEED SOMETHING NEW! SOMETHING FRESH!
CAN WE GO TO PARIS? PLEASE, MUMMY?
VERONICA, THAT SEEMS A BIT EXTRAVAGANT!
ALTHOUGH, I HAVEN'T BEEN ON A PARIS SHOPPING SPREE IN A WHILE...
GALLERIES LAMARDIE
THAT'S THE SPIRIT! LET'S HAVE SOME QUALITY MOM AND DAUGHTER TIME!
WELL, WHY NOT? LET ME CHECK WITH YOUR FATHER.
HIRAM, WE--
HERE'S THE CREDIT CARD. HAVE A GOOD TIME!
SUPERCHARGE
HIRAM LODGE

WOW! THAT WAS EASY! WHAT GIVES?
WHEN IT'S ONE OF YOU, I HAVE A FIGHTING CHANCE.
WHEN THE TWO OF YOU TEAM UP, I KNOW IT'S TIME TO GIVE IT UP!
HAVE A GREAT TIME!
MOULIN ROUGE
HOW DOES THIS LOOK?
BEAUTIFUL, DEAR!
THIS IS NICE...
Hmm... NOT BAD!
$3,000

WOW! WE SHOPPED ALL DAY!
BUT WE DIDN'T FIND THE PERFECT PROM DRESS... YET!
LOOKS LIKE THAT'LL BE TOMORROW'S JOB.
IT'S A TOUGH JOB, BUT SOMEONE'S GOT TO DO IT!
BACK IN RIVERDALE...
WHERE'S RON?
SHE WENT TO PARIS WITH HER MOM.
I BET SHE'S SHOPPING FOR THE PROM!
SHE'S GOING TO WANT TO OUTSHINE US ALL!
Er-- WHERE'S SHE STAYING?
PROBABLY "LE CHATEAU ROUGE." THAT'S HER FAVORITE HOTEL!
Eat at POP'S
WHY DO YOU ASK?
NO REASON...

I'VE GOT TO KEEP TABS ON HER!
LET'S SEE... WE LIVED IN PARIS FOR AWHILE WHEN WE MOVED FROM RIVERDALE...
I KNOW! I'LL CALL MY FRIEND SOPHIE!
SO...
YOU WANT ME TO SPY ON YOUR FRIEND?
YES! SHE'S STAYING AT "LE CHATEAU ROUGE."
I'M E-MAILING YOU A PHOTO OF HER.
ALL I WANT YOU TO DO IS THIS...
FOLLOW HER SHOPPING. WHEN SHE BUYS ANY FANCY DRESSES, TAKE A PICTURE OF IT AND E-MAIL IT TO ME!
WHY DON'T YOU DO THIS?
MY CASH FLOW ISN'T WHAT IT USED TO BE...
BESIDES, THIS'LL BE MUCH FASTER!

THE NEXT DAY...
BOY! THIS GIRL LIKES TO TALK!
OHMIGOSH! I'VE FOUND IT!
THAT'S THE DRESS!
COME ON! I WANT TO TRY IT ON!
IT'S BEAUTIFUL, VERONICA! I THINK WE'VE FOUND A WINNER!
I'LL TAKE IT!
SNAP
CLICK!
HEY, WHY IS THAT GIRL SNAPPING A PICTURE OF ME?
Er--uh--I LOVE THAT DRESS SO MUCH! I WANT TO SHOW IT TO MY MOTHER!
WELL, I CAN'T BLAME YOU!
SOON...
Ah-HA! THIS IS GREAT! SOPHIE SENT ME SOME GREAT SHOTS!
8

NOW TO FIND SOMEONE TO MAKE AN EXACT COPY OF THIS DRESS FOR ME!
I KNOW A GREAT SEAMSTRESS BACK IN PEMBROKE. I'LL CALL HER!
A FEW DAYS LATER...
HI, VERONICA! HOW WAS PARIS?
GREAT!
DID YOU BUY ANYTHING... LIKE A PROM DRESS?
WHAT? THAT WASN'T EVEN ON MY MIND.
Ah, PARIS... I LOVE PARIS!
HAVE YOU GOT A PROM DRESS, CHERYL?
YES. JUST SOME SIMPLE FROCK.
AND YOU, BETTY?
THE SAME DRESS I WORE LAST YEAR.
GOOD OL' PRACTICAL BETTY!

PROM NIGHT...
I LOOK STUNNING!
MOUTHS WILL DROP WHEN I WALK IN!
MOUTHS ARE DROPPING, ALL RIGHT!
GASP!
GASP!
THAT'S BECAUSE YOU'RE BOTH WEARING THE SAME DRESS!
GAK!!!
HOW?!
JUST SOMETHING I GOT AT MAL-MART!
I DON'T KNOW HOW YOU DID IT! THIS IS A ONE-OF-A-KIND DESIGNER DRESS!
WAIT! THAT GIRL WITH THE CAMERA PHONE!
YOU SPIED ON ME!
I HAVE FRIENDS ALL OVER THE GLOBE!
10

OH, WHOOPS! I TORE THAT SASH!
FORGIVE ME!
I TORE YOUR DRESS! MY BAD!
THAT'S IT! YOU TWO COOL OFF OUTSIDE! AND DON'T COME BACK UNTIL YOU DO!
LEARN HOW TO ACT LIKE PROPER YOUNG LADIES!
LOOK WHAT YOU DID! THIS IS ALL YOUR FAULT!
WELL, WE CERTAINLY MADE SOMEONE LOOK GOOD TONIGHT.
Huh?!
BETTY, YOU LOOK BEAUTIFUL TONIGHT!
OH, THIS OLD THING?
CHALK UP ONE FOR GOOD OL' PRACTICAL BETTY!
End

A Tale of Two
PROMS
Dan Parent

Betty and Veronica in "A Tale of 2 Proms"

ARCHIE! COME HERE!!
NO, ARCHIE, COME HERE!!
WHY DO I FEEL LIKE A PUPPET?
LET GO OF HIM, BETTY!
YOU FIRST, YOU PAIN IN THE NECK!
TIME OUT!!
I'LL BE OVER HERE WHILE YOU TWO CHILDREN CALM DOWN!
WOW! ARCHIE LOOKS FED UP FOR ONCE!!
WHAT'S WRONG, RED? I'M CHARLENE!
HI! I GO THROUGH THIS ALL THE TIME WITH MY GIRLFRIENDS!
I HAVE A SOLUTION TO YOUR PROBLEM!
WHAT'S THAT?

I GO TO CENTERVILLE HIGH!
COME TO MY PROM WITH ME!!
HEY, WHY NOT?!
THIS'LL SHOW THEM THEY CAN'T TREAT ME LIKE AN OBJECT!
EXCUSE ME, GIRLS! MEET CHARLENE, MY DATE FOR THE PROM!
WHAT?!
WE'LL BE ATTENDING THE PROM IN CENTERVILLE!
GOOD DAY!
I CAN'T BELIEVE IT!
HOW DARE HE SKIP OUT ON RIVERDALE'S OWN PROM?!
HOW COULD HE TURN DOWN TWO GIRLS LIKE US?
GEE, I WONDER!

ON PROM NIGHT...
GEE, YOU GIRLS LOOK SO BORED!!
WE ARE!
IT WAS TOO LATE FOR US TO GET A DATE FOR TONIGHT!
WE GET TO STAND HERE AND WATCH JUGHEAD PIG OUT!!
AT CENTERVILLE HIGH...
ARE YOU HAVING FUN, ARCHIE?
OH, YEAH, SURE!
YOU SEEM PREOCCUPIED!
I WAS JUST THINKING ABOUT SOMETHING...
GEE, I DON'T KNOW ANYBODY HERE!!
AND CHARLENE KEEPS GETTING DISTRACTED BY ALL HER FRIENDS!!
I WONDER WHAT THE GIRLS ARE DOING NOW...
I WONDER WHAT ARCHIE'S DOING NOW...
4

I'VE NEVER MISSED A RIVERDALE EVENT BEFORE!
AND I'M NOT GOING TO START NOW!
SORRY, CHARLENE! I GOTTA GO!
H-HUH?
IT'LL TAKE ME 45 MINUTES TO GET BACK TO RIVERDALE!!
IF I'M LUCKY I'LL MAKE IT BACK FOR THE LAST 10 MINUTES OR SO!
OH, NO! IT'S RAINING!
THIS'LL SLOW ME DOWN!!
LATER...
THE PROM'S ALMOST OVER! WHAT A DUD OF AN EVENING!
I KNOW!! I ACTUALLY BRIBED JUGHEAD WITH A BURGER TO DANCE WITH ME!!

OKAY, EVERYONE! GET READY FOR OUR LAST DANCE!
DID HE SAY LAST DANCE?!
ARCHIE!!
YOU LOOK LIKE A DROWNED RAT!!
AN ADORABLE DROWNED RAT!
SHALL WE HAVE THIS LAST DANCE?
YOU BET!
ISN'T IT NICE WHEN YOU GIRLS SHARE?
WE'LL NEVER FIGHT OVER YOU AGAIN!!
HA! HA! I CAN'T BELIEVE SHE SAID THAT WITH A STRAIGHT FACE!
The End